Just Plain Bob

Turning Mommies Wild:
The Carriage
Tales

Conversion Erotica

WARNING

This book contains sexually explicit scenes and adult language. It may be considered offensive to some readers. This book is for sale to adults ONLY.

Please store your files wisely where they cannot be accessed by underage readers.

* * * * * * * * * * * * * * * * * *

WANT FREE COPIES OF MY BOOKS?
Just visit my blog and download free copies of my books:
awesomeauthors.org/justplainbob

Copyright © 2015 by Just Plain Bob

All Rights reserved under International and Pan-American Copyright Conventions. By payment of required fees you have been granted the non-exclusive, non-transferable right to access and read the text of this book. No part of this text may be reproduced, transmitted, downloaded, decompiled, reverse-engineered or stored in or introduced into any information storage and retrieval system, in any form or by any means, whether electronic or mechanical, now known, hereinafter invented, without express written permission of 4Fun Publishing. For more information contact 4Fun Publishing. The publisher does not have any control over and does not assume any responsibility for author or third-party websites or their content. This book is a work of fiction. The characters, incidents and dialogue are drawn from the author's imagination and are not to be construed as real. While reference might be made to actual historical events or existing locations, the names, characters, places and incidents are either products of the author's imagination or are used fictitiously, and any resemblance to actual persons living or dead, business establishments, events or locales is entirely coincidental.

About the Publisher

4Fun Publishing, a member of **BLVNP Incorporated**, 340 S. Lemon #6200, Walnut CA 91789, info@blvnp.com / legal@blvnp.com

NOTE: Due to the highly emotional reaction of some people to works of erotic fiction, any email sent to the above address that contains foul language or religious references is automatically deleted by our anti-spam software and will not be seen. All other communications are welcome.

DISCLAIMER

Please don't be stupid and kill yourself. This book is a work of FICTION. Do not try any new sexual practice that you find in this book. It is fiction and not to be confused with reality. Neither the author nor the publisher or its associates assume any responsibility for any loss, injury, death or legal consequences resulting from acting on the contents in this book. Every character in this book is over 18 years of age. The author's opinions are not to be construed as the opinions of the publisher. The material in this book is for entertainment purposes ONLY. Enjoy.

Turning Mommies Wild:
The Carriage Tales
Conversion Erotica

By: Just Plain Bob

© **Just Plain Bob 2015**
ISBN: 978-1-68030-466-4

Chapter 1

Okay, I admit it - I'm fucked up. As well as being a pervert I've found out that I'm a cum-freak, but more on that later. I work midnights and so I'm around the house during the day when all the young housewives and mothers are out pushing their babies around in baby carriages and strollers. My greatest pleasure, my biggest kick, is turning those sweet young and innocent married women into gangbang-loving sluts. Hey, everyone has a jones, right? Mine just happens to be a little more perverse than most.

It started out innocently enough. Sandy was twenty-two and the mother of two babies, both toddlers, and one morning as I was working in my front yard, she came by pushing her two little ones in a baby carriage. Being neighborly I said good morning and made some small talk about the nice weather we were having and then she said that she'd heard that I had a pond and a waterfall in my backyard. I told her I did and I asked her if she wanted to see it. She said yes, that she would like to and a couple of minutes later we were setting on my deck, sipping coffee, and watching the Koi playing under the waterfall.

She was still there half an hour later when my buddy Tyrone stopped by. Tyrone is a big black dude that has a way with the ladies and pretty soon he and Sandy were chatting away like old friends. After Sandy was gone, Ty told me that he would sure like to tap her fresh young pussy and I laughed at him, "Dream on, Ty, dream on."

"No man, I mean it. Get her back here tomorrow and I'll see to it that we both tear off a piece of that fine ass."

"Just how do you figure you can do that?"

"Trust me on this one, dude. Tomorrow her sweet young pussy is ours."

The next morning I was sitting at my widow watching for Sandy to come up the street. About nine, I saw her heading my way and so I got outside and was working in the yard when she got to my place. I said good morning and asked her if she'd like to join me on the rear deck for coffee. She said she'd love some coffee so I told her to go on around back and I went into the house to put the coffee on and to call Tyrone. Ten minutes he was there and he and Sandy picked up their conversation where they had left off the day previous. When Sandy's cup was empty, Ty got up and went inside to get her a refill. Sandy was leaning back in her lounge chair, looking at the waterfall and watching the fish play, "This is something I could learn to like on a daily basis. It is just so peaceful and refreshing."

"You are more than welcome any day. Even if I'm not here you can come through the side gate and make yourself at home."

"Thanks. I might just take you up on that."

Tyrone came back with her coffee and for the next fifteen or twenty minutes, we sat and talked. Then Sandy dropped her coffee cup and said, "I feel dizzy" and then she tried to get up. Ty got up and helped her over to the chaise lounge and helped her sit down. He looked over at me and winked as he took out his cell phone and made a call.

"It's ready. Hurry up and get your butts over here."

"What's that all about?"

"Just getting us some help, dude."

"What's going on here, Ty?"

"I slipped a quarter dose of Amtph in her coffee."

"What the hell is Amtph?"

You know my brother the chemist?"

"Yeah, I've met him."

"The company he works for was working on a cancer suppressing drug and they accidentally found a compound that acts like that old myth, Spanish Fly. He gives me a supply and I use it and report the results back to him. I'm field testing it so to speak. Based on my testing they may be able to find a market for it. What it does is make her want to fuck. A full dose would make her want to fuck for twelve to fourteen hours, but the dose I gave her will only make her want to go for three or four hours. The beauty of it is when the Ampth wears off she will still want to fuck."

"We can't do this, man. She'll call the cops."

"No she won't. She's aware of what's going on. She is going to want every inch we can give her and then some. Once she starts begging for cock, we tape it and then warn her against telling anybody what happened. She can't tell her husband unless she wants him to know she is a cock-crazy slut and if she does tell him and he comes looking to kick ass we show him the tape and tell him to back off or we will let the whole world see what a slut his wife and the mother of his kids is."

"I don't know, Ty. It sounds like we are flirting with jail time here."

"Too late, my man. I told you she was aware and wants it, right? We have to follow through."

"What was the phone call?"

"Got some help coming. I want her so sexually stimulated that she behaves like a sex maniac while I tape her. You want to be first?"

***

Actually I really did want to be first, but just then the younger of Sandy's two babies started to cry. I finally figured out she was hungry and I searched through the bag hanging on the back of the baby carriage and found a full bottle of something that I figured was baby formula. I ended up feeding Sandy's baby while watching Tyrone feed Sandy his cock. I found out as I watched that I got a huge charge out of seeing black on white. I had the baby on my shoulder burping her when the help that Ty had called arrived. I knew a couple of them and I was not surprised that they were all black. One that I didn't know looked at me with a smirk on his face, "Who's the wimpy white dude? Her hubby? He get off on seeing his pretty little white wife turned into a nigger-loving slut?"

"What the fuck, Ty? You invited this racist asshole into my home?"

"Shut the fuck up, Derek. He is our host and my friend and that's all the fuck you need to know."

Just then the baby burped and I said, "That's right, sweetie, you tell him" and everybody laughed.

On the chaise lounge, Tyrone was slamming his cock into Sandy's tender young pussy. Her head rolled from side to side and her arms were grabbing at Ty's back and her legs kept trying to wrap around him. Ty looked over his shoulder and said, "Somebody get ready. I'm close to shooting and we have to keep her going."

Everybody stripped and when Ty gave a grunt and held himself still for a moment we knew he had cum. He pulled himself off Sandy and I didn't get to be next because I was changing the baby's diaper and I didn't get to be third either because I was feeding Sandy's other baby. When it was time for the fourth man to climb into the saddle, I was changing diapers again. I told the guys to carry her into the house and take her up to the bedroom while I put her two kids down for a nap.

When I finally got my turn, Sandy was starting to look glassy eyed. As I sank my cock into her hot, wet and no longer tight little box, I almost came. It felt so incredibly good. I would never have believed that I could find sloppy sixths so exciting. Sandy was moaning I was pounding into her as hard as I could when suddenly she arched her back and cried out, "Oh fuck!" and Tyrone laughed and said, "Way to go, white boy, you made her cum" and all the others cheered me on. I lasted another two minutes and then I came.

Ty was next and as he banged into her, she gave a loud moan and her legs came up and she dug her heels into the back of Tyrone's legs and he laughed, "Now is when it gets good. We will give you lots of climaxes baby. You will be going home well satisfied today."

After Ty and Derek mounted her, she was begging for more cock and for Derek to fuck her harder. For the next hour she never went more than ten seconds without a cock in her. I had her two more times and then I heard the babies fussing and I went to check on them. I changed some diapers, fed and burped both of them again and put them back down to nap. When I got back to the bedroom, they had Sandy on her hands and knees and she had Derek's cock in her mouth and Devon buried in her ass. I could hear the moans coming out of her mouth around Derek's cock and she was pushing her ass back at Devon as he plowed into her. When Devon came and pulled out of her I moved behind her and slid my cock in her ass. Just like when I'd gotten her pussy the feeling was fantastic and I wondered how "sloppy seconds" had ever become a derisive term. I loved it and I began to think that it would be the way I'd like to go from then on.

Sammy had cum in her mouth and moved away and Hal stepped up to push his cock in. Sandy reached out and grabbed it and pulled him to her open hole as she was slamming her ass back at me and crying," "Oh God, oh God, Oh God." It went on for another half hour and then they guys said they had to be going and they dressed and left. Sandy was lying on the bed and crying, "Please, please somebody do me please?" Ty looked at me and shook his head no and I couldn't get me up again either, but I couldn't stand to see Sandy suffer like that.

"Ty, are we tight?"

"You know we are man."

"Then this is just between us. No one ever gets to know what a sick puppy I really am, okay?"

"What are you going to do?"

"Help her out."

I knelt down between Sandy's legs and started to eat her cum smeared sopping wet pussy. Her hands grabbed the back of my head as I sucked on her clit and she hunched up at my mouth and moaned, cried, screamed and hollered as I brought her to one very large orgasm. Then she fell back on the bed and in minutes she was lightly snoring. I looked down at her and was amazed at what I had done. I had buried my face in a cunt full of other men's cum, sucked it up and I had loved every second of it.

Tyrone and I stood looking down at her. She still looked young and innocent, but she was a mess. There were no marks on her - we had warned everyone about that - but her cunt lips were red and swollen and she had dried cum all over her.

"I'll put on a pot of coffee and then we will have to get her cleaned up and out of here. I'm all out of baby food and clean diapers."

***

The shower woke Sandy up and we toweled her off and poured coffee into her and then we left her in the bedroom to get dressed. When she came out, Ty and I were in the living room watching the tape that had been made of our little party.

"What are you going to do with that?"

"Nothing, sweetie. Just keep it as a memento of a very nice day. I'll make you a copy if you would like."

Sandy surprised the hell out of us when she said, "No, thanks. If I want to see it I can always come here."

No "why did you do this to me?" No "I'll get even with you bastards" or "I'll make you pay for this" just a matter of fact "I can always come here." Tyrone and I looked at each other in stunned disbelief as Sandy loaded up her two babies and left.

When Ty was ready to leave, I walked him to the door and as he walked out on the porch, Helen was walking by pushing her baby buggy. I waved at her and she waved back and Tyrone said, "Let's do her next."

Chapter 2

When Tyrone said, "Let's do her next" as Helen walked down the street, he caught me by surprise. I figured that what we had done with Sandy was a one-time thing. "Wait here" Tyrone said, "I'll be right back." He came back a moment later and handed me a bottle with an eyedropper in it. "You need to dose their coffee as soon as you get them in the backyard and then call me on my cell and I'll take it from there."

I spent all that day waiting for a cop car to pull up in front of my house. When that didn't happen, I braced myself for a visit from Sandy's outraged husband and when that didn't happen either, I began to think that maybe we had gotten away with it. But I was still shaky enough that I didn't make a move on Helen for a couple of days. I had no idea how I was going to get Helen in the backyard, I thought about it for two days before deciding that simple usually works best. I made sure that I was working in the yard when she came by on Thursday morning.

"Hey, Helen, got a minute?"

"What's up?"

"I need a woman's perspective on something. My ex-wife always told me that I always seemed to see things out of balance."

"What is it?"

"I'm working on my rock garden and pond and I don't know that I'm happy with the way my waterfall comes into the pond. I'd like another opinion."

"I'd love to see it, but I don't know that my opinion will mean much."

I led her around to the back of the house and had her take a seat while I turned on the pump that ran the waterfall, then I offered her coffee and she said she'd love some and I went into the house and got her a cup. I dosed it per Tyrone's instructions and then I called him on his cell. He told me he would be over in ten minutes and the rest of the guys would be there maybe twenty minutes after that. I took the coffee out to Helen and by then the waterfall was up and running. "What do you think?"

"I think I'll leave my husband and move in with you. I could sit here all day and soak up sunshine and listen to the water. I wouldn't change a thing as far as the pond and waterfall are concerned, but if it were mine, I'd get some more oranges and yellows down near this end of the rock garden. The reds are a bit overwhelming, but then again, that's just me. I'm partial to orange and yellow."

We talked more about flowers and I asked her what she would use and she named off several of her favorites and we discussed them and then I noticed her give her head a little shake and she opened and closed her eyes a couple of times.

"Are you all right?"

"I think so, I just felt a little dizzy there for a moment."

I looked at my watch and saw that it had been twenty-three minutes since she took her first sip of coffee. She saw me check my watch and I saw comprehension appear in her eyes, "You bastard! You drugged me with something,"

I smiled at her, "Yes I did, sweetie, and I think you are going to love the outcome."

She dropped the coffee cup (I made a mental note to get some unbreakable ones) and she shook her head and then she stood up and walked toward me. Tyrone showed up just as she went to her knees in front of me and reached for my zipper. "Come on, Helen," I said, "Let's take this to the bedroom."

While Ty undressed her, I went down and got six-month-old Sasha and brought her upstairs. Sasha was sleeping, at least for now, and I put her down in a corner of the room. Ty and I stood looking down at Helen and appreciating the view. Her tits were huge and stuck up like mountain peaks and she had a bald pussy. I could see her eyes watching us, trying to figure out why we weren't taking advantage to what she was so willing to give us.

Ty said, "You first today."

I ran a finger along her slit and then I worked it into her. She was tight, way too tight. I got up and got some KY and worked on her a bit and then I moved between her legs. It took me several minutes to work my cock all the way into her pussy and then I started fucking her. She was tight and it was okay, but I knew that I was going to enjoy her more after the other guys got there and I could get my sloppy whatever. I came and got out of the way so Tyrone could have at her. He banged away at her for several minutes before cumming and then I mounted her again. It was a lot better my second time because she had my first load and Ty's donation in her. I had no idea why all of a sudden, after twelve years of fucking girls, I was so in love with cum-filled pussies, but there was no denying that I was.

I had just cum for my second time when the baby started fussing. I checked Sasha and found that her diaper was dry so I looked through the diaper bag for a bottle and then I picked her up and fed her. When she wouldn't take anymore, I put her on my shoulder and patted her she burped and then I rocked her until she went to sleep.

Tyrone was nearing his climax and Helen was moaning when I got back to the bedroom. I heard the front door open and a voice call out "We're here." Tyrone hollered back for them to come on up, "And hurry. We need some help." Derek and four other guys came into the bedroom and immediately started to strip.

I glance over at them and said, "Tyrone is almost ready to shoot and when he gets out of the way, I need one of you to get right on so we can keep her going.

"Here it comes, honey," Ty said and a moment later he pulled away from Helen and Devon rolled her over and pushed into her from behind. Hal stepped up and fed his cock into Helen's mouth and held her head and began to fuck her face. I thought I heard the baby and I went to check on her, but she was sleeping peacefully.

When I got back to the bedroom, Helen was pretty much behaving like a screaming nymphomaniac. She was sitting on Derek's cock, sucking on Tyrone's bone and Devon was behind her getting ready to enter her asshole. Devon was playing with her hanging tits and every once in a while a bit of milk would squirt out. I stood and watched as Ty came in her mouth and was replaced by Jason, who was replaced by Stan. Then Derek came and crawled out from under her. Hal looked at me and I shook my head no, "I'm waiting for her asshole."

"Get ready then, I'm almost ready to pop," Devon said and I got ready to take his place. He grunted and said, "There you go, baby" and as he pulled out a stream of cum flowed out of Helen's ass. I immediately filled the hole and good god did it feel great. Helen was really into it and even with a cock in her mouth I could hear her screaming, "Fuck me, fuck me, fuck me, goddamn you, fuck me."

I don't know if it was me in her ass, Hal in her pussy or Stan in her mouth or a combination, but Helen had three orgasms before I came in her ass. I got out of the way and Ty took my place. He slammed his cock in her and she squealed and had another orgasm.

I left the room and went to check on Sasha. She was sleeping soundly and I adjusted the blankets around her and then went downstairs to get a cold drink. When I hit the bottom of the stairs, I happened to look out the front window and I saw Sandy coming up the street. She slowed down when she got to the front of the house, looked like she was hesitating, and then she went on by. I wondered what that was about.

When I got back to the bedroom, the boys had changed positions. Derek was lying on the bed and Helen was sitting on his cock and bouncing up and down on him. It wasn't until Stan got on the bed and pushed her backward so the her back was almost on Derek's chest that I realized that Derek had his stick up Helen's ass. Stan lined his cock up with Helen's cunt and with one push shoved it home. Helen screamed out, "Oh fuck" and then she began to cry, "Oh god, oh god, oh god, so good, so fucking good" and then she had an orgasm. I pulled a chair next to the bed and stood on it and then I leaned forward and supported myself by putting my hands on the bedpost. My cock was only three inches from Helen's face, but in my position I couldn't get any closer. Then, God bless her, Helen turned her head, saw my cock and leaned over and started sucking it.

Three minutes later Stan said, "I'm going to blow. Who wants next on her cunt?"

"Me" I said and I pulled out of Helen's mouth, which got me a nasty look, and got off the chair. Stan dismounted and I took his place. As my dick slid into her I almost came it felt so good. It was my first time in her pussy since the other guys had arrived and I had no idea how many loads I was soaking in, but it felt divine. I made up my mind, right then and there, that if I ever got married again my wife was going to have to be a gangbang-loving slut.

I didn't even try to fuck Helen at first. I just held myself in her and soaked my cock in her hot, wet cunt and felt the sensations of Derek's cock rubbing against mine as he pounded up into her ass. Then I looked around and saw other's waiting and so I began banging away. Nobody had a cock in Helen's mouth so her words weren't muffled as she just kept crying, "Fuck me, make me cum, fuck me hard, please make me cum."

Two minutes later, Derek said, "Here it comes, you cum-hungry slut" and I felt his cock throb as it touched mine through the thin membrane and that sent me over the edge and I blew my load into Helen's cunt. Helen, who had been crying "make me cum, make me cum" suddenly screamed out "Make me cummmmmmmm" and her whole body shook like a dog shitting peach pits. She was still shaking when I pulled out and Devon took my place.

I went to check on Sasha again and I saw she was starting to fidget. I checked her diaper and found that she needed to be changed. I put a clean diaper on her, put her pacifier in her mouth and then rocked her back to sleep. When I got back to the bedroom, I found Helen crying, "No, not yet, please don't leave, not yet" and I looked around and saw that Derek and Devon were getting dressed to go. "Please" Helen begged, "Please, just once more each, just once more." The two looked at each other and then undressed. I watched for another hour as the guys rotated from mouth to pussy to ass and then Derek and Devon did something that blew me away. They fucked Helen in her pussy at the same time - she had two cocks in her pussy! - and Helen went crazy. She screamed, hollered, yelled and had another orgasm. I looked over at Ty, "You and me next?"

"Shit yes, man, I got to try that."

When Derek and Devon were done, Ty and me took their place. First I fucked her for a bit and then stayed still while Ty fucked her and then we just kept taking turns until Ty came and pulled out. With Ty gone, I pushed Helen back on the bed and fucked her as hard as I could until I came. I got up to go to the bathroom and Tyrone got on the bed.

When I got back to the bedroom, Ty was lying on his back and Helen was kneeling over him sucking him off. I had a choice - ass or pussy - and I said, "Fuck it, why not both?" I moved up behind her and slid into her wet pussy and she pushed back at me and moaned around Tyrone's cock. After five minutes I pulled out of her and she cried out, "No, don't stop, not yet damn it" but the cries stopped when I pushed myself into her ass. She started squealing and I started fucking her butt as hard as I could. It took me almost ten minutes to cum and by then Ty had cum and had gone off to shower. Helen was telling me to fuck her, "Make me cum, you bastard. Fuck my ass, make me cum one more time." She did and then I did and then I fell down on the bed next to her almost exhausted.

Helen fell forward on the bed and then she rolled over and the two of us were lying next to each other, breathing hard and looking up at the ceiling. Then I rolled over and went down on her and sucked the juices of seven men out of her cunt. She kicked and screamed and held my head against her box until she had an orgasm and I'd had enough. After maybe a minute of silence Helen said, "You are a miserable, no good, rotten bastard for drugging me, but I'm glad that you did. I haven't felt this fucking satisfied since my last frat party gangbang in college."

Ty had come into the room and he said, "So you are no stranger to gangbangs?"

"God no. I was the biggest slut on campus for four years. I'd forgotten how much I loved it. What did you plan on doing with the tape, blackmail me into doing it again?"

"Kind of. Not blackmail you into doing it again, not that we would mind doing it again, but to by your silence."

"How's that?"

"The theory is that we show you loving it and tell you if you tell your husband and he comes looking for us every one of your neighbors and relatives gets a copy showing you begging for it."

"Well you won't need it for that. What I want to know is when can we do it again?"

"You want to do it again?"

"Fuck yeah!"

"You tell us when."

"I can't do it too often or my pussy would get so big that my hubby wouldn't be able to feel the sides and I don't dare let him find out. How about same time next week?"

Ty and I looked at each other and smiled.

***

Ty and I were sitting in the living room watching the tape of Sandy while Helen was taking a shower. We had intended to turn it off before Helen came in the room, but we were so wrapped up in it that we didn't hear when the shower was shut off. "Holy shit! I don't believe it." Helen had come into the room and had seen the tape and we hadn't heard her. "I just don't believe it. Little Miss Goody Two Shoes with a cock in every hole - that's just so priceless."

"You don't like her?"

"Oh I like her, it's just that everyone thinks she's the perfect mother, the perfect wife and the perfect little homemaker. It's just a shock to see that she is just as big a pig as I am. How many others have you done this with?"

"You are just the second," I said and Tyrone laughed, "And I hope you aren't the last."

"Maybe I can help you."

"What?"

"Maybe I can help you. My next-door neighbor Beverly is a little snot. I'd like to see her with a cock in every hole." She looked at me, "I noticed that with the exception of you all the others were black. Is there some significance in that?"

"No, not really. Those were just the ones Ty could reach on short notice."

"Can you get some Mexicans?"

"I suppose, why?"

"Beverly and her husband hate Mexicans. They are always harping on how the "fucking spics" are taking all the jobs and ruining the economy. I would love to see her fucked silly by a couple of dozen of them."

I looked at Ty and he looked back at me and shrugged, "I don't know about that many, but I can probably come up with three or four. How does she feel about blacks?"

"I'm not sure, but if she is that rabid about Mexicans I can't imagine that she is overly fond of blacks."

"Okay, we will get her a mixture. When do you want to do this?"

"The sooner the better. But for now I need to get out of here. I don't have any clean diapers for Sasha and I need to get home."

I walked her to the door and as she was leaving she said, "You are still an asshole, but you aren't a bad fuck. On days you aren't running a gangbang, could I stop by for a quickie or three?"

"What about your hubby?"

"Fuck him. You have that relaxing waterfall and you scratch an itch that he hasn't scratched in years to say nothing about the absolutely marvelous way you eat pussy."

"The gate to the backyard is never locked. Make yourself at home."

She kissed me and I watched as she headed on down toward her end of the street.

Chapter 3

I hit the Safeway on my way home from work and picked up some stuff that I never thought I would ever buy. Baby oil, baby powder, and diapers - Huggies and Pampers (I couldn't decide which was better so I got both) - and some baby bottles and formula. I wanted to be prepared for the next time I had a baby to deal with. When I got home, I saw a great-looking pair of legs sticking out in front of one of the deck chairs. Because of the high back, I couldn't tell who it was so I put the coffee on and when it was ready I poured it into a carafe and put it on a tray with two cups, cream and sugar and went out to see who my visitor might be.

As the door opened, a head looked around the chair and I saw that it was Sandy. As I set the tray down on the table in front of her, she looked up at me and said, "Is it safe to drink this time?" I poured myself a cup from the carafe and took a sip, "Life is just a series of taking chances, sweetie. I might be drugging myself to drug you, you'll never know unless you have a sip." She looked at me for several seconds and then she poured herself a cup, added cream and took a sip. She set the cup down and looked at me for several more seconds.

"I'll bet you are surprised to see me here."

I just looked at her and waited.

"Well, you can't be any more surprised than I am. I've spent the better part of the last week taking my walks in the other direction just to avoid coming past your house. Now I'm here and I don't know why. Do you know why I'm here?"

I thought about her question and then said, "No, not really. It could be one of several things. You could be worried about the tape we made and what we might do with it. You might be worried that none of the guys used condoms and that you might have been made pregnant or gotten a disease. I don't know about the pregnancy thing, but before we started to do this, Ty and all the guys had themselves tested, for our sake as much as yours. Maybe you just want to watch the tape. You did say before you left that if you wanted to see it you could always come here to do it. And while I admit that it is a remote possibility, you may have come here to ask if you can do it again."

"How about all of the above except for the last one."

"Where are the babies?"

"Sleeping in the shade over by the gate."

"Go get them and bring them inside while I set up the VCR."

After Sandy got the babies settled, she sat down next to me on the couch and I hit the play button and settled back to watch Sandy watch herself.

I watched for ten minutes as she went from calm and curious to hot and bothered. First it was a hand to her breast and I watched as she slowly began to caress it. Then it was shifting and opening her legs and dropping a hand to rub her mound. Then came the heavy breathing and the hard rubbing. I didn't even think she knew I was there anymore. Just to see I took out my rapidly hardening cock and just sat there with it standing straight up and waving in the air. Several minutes went by and then I saw her glance over and see it. She quickly turned her head back to the TV and then for the next two minutes she would glance over and quickly turn away. Then, with a sudden "Oh God" she turned and her head went down into my lap and her mouth swallowed my dick.

I just sat there and let her give me a blow job for several minutes and then I reached out and took the bottom of her tee shirt and pulled it up until I could get to her bra straps. I unsnapped the bra and then I reached under it and cupped her tit in my hand and started rolling the nipple between my fingers and she moaned. I pushed her away from me and she got a hurt look on her face. I pushed her back on the couch and started to pull her shorts down and the hurt look changed to one of lust. As soon as her shorts and panties were off, she spread her legs wide and moaned, "Hurry, please hurry."

I pushed my cock at her hole and she was tight, very tight and I pulled back from her and went down on her. In less than a minute she had her hands wound in my hair and was pulling my face into her cunt even as she pushed it up at my face. I kept at her until I thought she was wet enough and then I moved back up. When the head of my cock split her pussy she grabbed my ass and her nails bit into me. To hell with going slow I thought and I rammed my cock into her until my pubic bone hit hers and then I started fucking her as hard as I could. Her heels were drumming against the back of my legs and her head was rolling from side to side as she made noises that defy description. Whatever they were, I knew that it meant that she was really into it and so was I. Unfortunately I was too into it and I came before I really wanted to. She wasn't near ready and she cried out "No, not yet, please not yet" as I pulled out of her. I quickly went down on her and began to slurp my cum out of her cunt as I tried to get her off with my mouth. I worked hard at it until I was rewarded by her grabbing my hair and pulling me into her pussy while she screamed and came loud enough to wake up her sleeping babies. I nibbled on her clit as I waited for her to come down from her high and then I pulled away from her so she could get up and go take care of her crying kids.

It was about twenty minutes later when she walked back into the bedroom and as I watched her approach my cock started to rise up.

"Oh my, ready already? It takes my husband almost half an hour before he can go again."

I didn't point out that it had been almost that long since I came in her. If she wanted to think I was a stud, who was I to deny it? I reached up and pulled her down to me and kissed her. Our tongues dueled for a bit and then Sandy broke the kiss, "This is wrong, I shouldn't be doing this. I love my hus…" and I shut her up by kissing her again and shoving my tongue in her mouth. Then I slid my hand down her naked belly and used my fingers on her pussy to try and build a fire again. She moaned and her tongue darted into my mouth and in a minute she was squirming against my hand. I broke the kiss and got up from the couch and pulled her after me as I walked around behind the couch. I bent her forward over the back of the couch and entered her from behind. I fucked her slowly for several minutes to get my cock nice and wet and then I pulled out of her cunt and pushed myself slowly into her ass. She hissed out a "Yesssssss" as I worked my way in and then I started to fuck her nice and easy.

Sandy was moaning as my dick worked back and forth in her ass and then the moans turned to crying. I looked down and saw tears running down her cheeks. Alarmed, I stopped fucking her and she cried out, "No, don't stop, please don't stop."

"Why are you crying, am I hurting you?"

"No, just fuck me, please, honey, please just fuck my ass."

"What's wrong?"

"Nothing, everything. This is wrong, I love my husband, but I can't stop thinking about the other day and what I did and how much I loved it."

I slowed down and was just doing a slow back and forth so she could talk. I liked where this seemed to be going."

"It's wrong, so wrong, I love Barry and yet I gloried in being a fuck-crazy slut. God help me I loved it, I loved it and I want to do it again. It's wrong, but I've never felt so alive in my life. It's wrong and I shouldn't be doing this, but I can't help myself."

"Should I call Tyrone?"

She didn't answer so I stopped stroking into her and said, "Sandy, do you want me to call Tyrone?"

She was silent for a second and then she moaned, "Yes, please call Tyrone."

"Anyone else?"

This time the answer came just a little quicker, "Maybe one or two more."

I smiled to myself as I picked up the pace and pounded her asshole. I came and left her still bent over the couch as I went to the bathroom to wash off my dick and then I got my cell phone and made the call.

***

It was two in the afternoon before Sandy left to go home. Tyrone had managed to round up three other guys on short notice and the five of us banged Sandy for almost four hours. Between bouts with Sandy's mouth, pussy and ass, I had to feed and change Sandy's two kids and I was starting to feel like I should advertise myself as a baby sitter. The last thing I did before Sandy left was go down on her and try to suck all the goo out of her and just like the first time she went nuts on me and got me so excited that I had to fuck her one more time.

As Sandy was pushing her baby carriage down the street, I asked Ty how long he thought it would last before her husband caught on to what was happening. "Don't know, dude, but I hope it's a long, long time. We still on for tomorrow?"

"Far as I know. Helen said to plan on nine o'clock. Can you have everybody here by eight-thirty? She doesn't want to waste a lot of time."

"We still have to wait ten minutes for the Ampth to kick in."

"Yeah, but only on Bev. Helen won't be taking any and she wants to go as soon as she gets here."

"I'll see what I can do, my man, I'll just have to see what I can do."

Chapter 4

I was sitting on the deck sipping coffee and tossing Koi sticks to the fish in the pond when I heard, "Hello there, neighbor, is the coffee pot on?"

I turned and saw Helen with a rather plain-looking young woman. Kind of plain in the face, but it looked like she had world class tits under her sweatshirt. Helen introduced me to Bev and I asked them if they would like some coffee and both said yes. I went into the kitchen and poured the coffee and doctored Bev's and then I went to the bottom of the stairs and hollered up to Ty and the boys that the girls had arrived. Upstairs waiting for the word were five Mexicans, four blacks, two Arabs and one Asian. A regular United Nations and then of course there was me - the token white boy.

I took the coffee outside and as the girls sipped theirs, we talked about the weather, gossiped about the neighbors and made general small talk. After about ten minutes, Helen asked me to keep an ear out for Sasha while she used the bathroom. Eight minutes later, Bev was looking at my crotch and licking her lips. I got up and went inside and called up to Tyrone and told him to hurry down because I was going to need some help. In the background I could hear, "Oh yes, just like that" as Helen got off to her early start.

Tyrone, Derek and two of the Mexicans came downstairs just as Bev took my cock in her mouth. I was pleased to see that Bev did indeed have a marvelous-looking rack hidden under her sweatshirt. Actually, she had a magnificent body hidden underneath her loose clothing. One of the Mexicans laid down on the chaise lounge and the other three picked Bev up and lowered her face down into his lap and then Derek and Tyrone held her while Carlos entered her from behind. I got the camera and started taping. I was shooting a close up of Carlos shoving his cock into Bev's hairless beaver when I caught movement out of the corner of my eye. I glanced that way and saw Sandy standing there watching. When she saw me looking at her, she blushed and then turned around and hurried away. I almost went after her but decided I'd best not, at least not until I found out how Helen felt about Sandy knowing about her.

When Juan and Carlos finished with Bev, Tyrone and Derek took her next while I taped and then Tyrone taped while I had Bev's super tight ass. After I came, the guys picked Bev up and carried her to the bedroom where Helen was already at play. I have a king-sized bed so there was plenty of room to put Bev down next to Helen. Helen had three cocks in her and the sight of the black cock being pushed in her white face along with her beautiful tits swinging and swaying as the other two guys in her holes fucked her got me hard all over again. I was set to shove my cock in Bev when I heard a noise - I had forgotten all about Sasha. Helen heard the baby too and she took her mouth off the cock she had been sucking long enough to look at me and say, "It's not time for her feeding so she must just have a wet diaper. I'm a little busy right now so would you please take care it?" I sighed, told my cock it would have to wait and went to take care of the baby and by the time I got back, all six holes were filled.

Bev was really into it when I got back. She had her legs wrapped tight around Manulito and her mouth clamped tight on Ramon while Carlos and Juan were each working on a tit. Ramon shot his load and as it came bubbling out of the corners of Bev's mouth he pulled away from her. Bev's head followed his cock as it left her to try and keep it and she only relaxed and laid back down when Francisco moved up to take Ramon's place. For the next two hours, it was just fuck and suck as all the guys took turns on Helen and Bev. Bev got to experience a couple of three-holers and once Carlos and Juan had their dicks in Bev's cunt at the same time.

Eventually the guys had to go and the fuckfest wound down. As soon as the last guy was gone, Helen straddled Bev's face and pushed her cum filled pussy down toward Bev's mouth. I got pissed and pulled Helen off of Bev, "Hey, that's supposed to be mine." I pushed Helen down on the bed and went down on her and sucked her cunt until she screamed and had an orgasm and then I rolled off her and went to work on Bev. Eating her out gave me a hard on so I moved up and slid my cock into Bev's sloppy pussy and she hissed out a low "yesssss" as I bottomed out. Everyone was gone so Helen could take care of Sasha and I could take my time and enjoy the feel of just soaking in Bev's hot swamp of a hole. I played with her world class tits as I slowly stroked in and out and she looked up at me.

Her rather plain face had taken on a certain lustful beauty and I had the thought that I wouldn't mind keeping her around for a while. Bev's eyes were looking into mine and every move made my in-stroke and our pubic bones met she hissed out a "yes…yes." I remembered what Helen had told about Bev's racial attitudes and I remembered how enthusiastic she had been while the Mexicans were fucking her and I couldn't resist a little teasing.

"Did you like all that Mexican dick, Bev? Did all that hard Spanish meat satisfy you? Did you like the feel of all that Chicano sperm splashing around inside you? Want to do it again, Bev? Want another Mexican gangbang? They loved your fantastic tits, sweetie, and they want more of you. Do you want more of them?"

Bev's nails dug deep into my ass and she arched up at me and screamed, "Yes, God damn it, yes!" as she had an orgasm. I had mine seconds later and then I rolled off her and lay on the bed trying to catch my breath while Helen pulled Bev off the bed and led her to the shower.

I was down in the basement when Helen and Bev left and I wondered what the two of them talked about on the way home. Did Bev realize that Helen had set her up, or did she think that I had drugged and taken advantage of both of them? I also wondered if her husband would be showing up at my door in the near future.

That evening I was in the basement when the doorbell rang. I looked up at the security monitor and saw Helen standing there. When I let her in she said, "Hubby's watching Sasha while I run to the store. Got time for a quickie before you have to go to work?" When we were done, I asked her how long before I could expect to see Bev's husband show up on my porch.

"Probably never. She's too scared to let him find out, she's afraid he would kill her. Did you know that both Carlos and Juan gave her their phone numbers? Do you know that she's going to ask you to set up another gangbang for her? I think we turned little Bev into a slut. Who else you want me to bring by?"

I laughed, "What are you, my new pimp?"

"No, I just think that every girl should have a chance to feel as good as I do when I have a lot of cocks to play with."

"Speaking of girls who like a lot of cocks to play with, while we were doing Bev on the back patio, Sandy came through the gate. I almost invited her to stay, but I didn't know how you would feel about that."

"Hell, lover, I don't mind. It will be just like college. Sandy, Bev and I can start a sorority for sluts. Hey, got to run to Safeway, see you tomorrow?"

"No. I've got my yearly physical tomorrow and then I have some errands to run. I'll be gone fishing this weekend so it will be Monday before you can stop by again."

"Okay, but if I have to wait that long you had better have some help when I get here."

Chapter 5

I would have been better off staying home over the weekend. The weather was lousy and the fishing sucked. Then at work Sunday night there was an accident that shut the line down for half an hour and then for the rest of the night the supervisors were total assholes as they pushed everyone to try and catch up.

When I got home I was surprised to find my driveway and the street in front of the house filled with cars. I'd forgotten about Helen having told me to make sure I had help on Monday morning. I'd set it up with Ty before leaving for the weekend and then had forgotten about it. I walked through the house and looked out onto the deck and I wasn't surprised to see Helen and the guys out there, but I was somewhat surprised to see Sandy out there also. When I unlocked the back door to the deck, I was greeted with yells of "It's about time" and "What kept you" and then everyone trooped into the house and headed for the bedroom. The girls stopped long enough to kiss me on the cheek and give me instructions. Helen said, "I'm weaning Sasha from breast feeding so there are three bottles in the diaper bag" and then Devon picked her up and carried her away. Next Sandy told me that the red bottles were for Mikey and the blue bottles were for Dawn and then she kissed me on the cheek again and ran after everyone else leaving me feeling like I was running a day care for sluts.

I did get a couple of blow jobs and a couple of fucks between feedings and diaper changes, but not near as many of either as I would have liked. I did get to do my favorite part and do a clean-up on both Helen's and Sandy's cream pies. Doing it gave me a hard on and then I had the unique experience of two women fighting over who would get it. Sandy won the coin toss and when we were done and I was lying on the bed between the two of them, they started talking about who they could bring in next. I immediately spoke up and put in my two cents worth. I told them it needed to be someone who didn't have any kids. "I'm tired of everyone else having all the fun while I'm stuck with feeding babies and changing diapers."

Sandy said, "I don't know anyone on the street without kids who doesn't work, do you?"

"Well" said Helen, "There is one, but I don't know if I can get her to come up here. I guess I can try."

"Well then, how about this. Next time, I'll watch the kids so you can fuck until you get tired and then you can watch them while I play, okay?"

Helen agreed and I said that it sounded like a plan. Sandy looked at her watch, "I've got time for one more if you can get it up." Helen laughed and said, "And I thought I was a slut."

***

Tuesday was uneventful, but on Wednesday the front doorbell rang and when I answered it I found a very nervous-looking Bev standing there.

"Can I come in?"

She kept looking around and I finally figured out that she was afraid she would be seen going into the house of the neighborhood bachelor. I stepped aside and let her in. I offered her coffee and she said no. She was looking around and she said, "Is anyone else here?"

When I said no, that I was alone I saw the disappointment on her face, "But I guess that I could make some calls." I took her by the hand and led her over to the couch. "Here, sit down next to me and show me how happy it would make you if I were to call some people." I took my cock out and waved it at her a couple of times. "Come on, Bev, show me how bad you want me to make some calls."

Bev looked down at my cock, back up at my face and then back down at my cock. I picked up my cell phone and showed it to her and she reached over and took hold of my cock and started stroking it.

I punched Tyrone's number into the phone and when he answered I said, "Ty, old buddy, Bev's here and she's unhappy that I'm alone. Can you help the poor girl out?" Then to Bev I said, "I am going to need some help, aren't I?" Bev moaned and started to work my cock faster. "And Ty, Bev is partial to hot Mexican cock, see what you can do for her, okay?" I disconnected and said, "That is what you wanted, isn't it?" She nodded her head yes. "Then show some appreciation girl - suck my cock."

Bev sucked me off twice and fucked me twice before Tyrone showed up. He had Derek and Devon with him and told us that Carlos, Manulito, Juan and Francisco were on the way. Bev was an insatiable fucking slut and for the next four hours, she was never without a cock in her somewhere. Around two-thirty the last of the guys left and I settled down to do my clean-up chores which only served to get me hard again and for the next hour it was repetition. Fuck Bev, suck Bev, get hard again and then do it all over again. Sometime around three forty-five Bev and I feel asleep.

***

I woke up and Bev was still in bed next to me. I glanced at the clock, saw that it was nine-thirty and I panicked. I grabbed Bev's shoulder and shook it. She was slow to wake up and I shook her again. She sat up and asked what was wrong and I told her we were in a shit load of trouble.

"Why?"

"Because it is almost ten o'clock! What are you going to tell your husband when you get home?"

"Nothing. He's not home. He's out of town and won't be home until tomorrow night."

"Don't you have to be there when he calls?"

"The cheap bastard never calls home when he's on a trip. He won't waste money on a long distance call." She reached down and put her hand on my cock, "But since we are awake do you suppose we could find something to do?"

I call in sick to work and then I called Tyrone and told him to stop by in the morning. "And Ty? Bev says please don't come alone."

It was the first time in six years that I'd had a woman in my bed all night, but I got damned little sleep.

Ty arrived at seven-twenty with Carlos, Juan and Francisco and Manulito showed up ten minutes later. I sent them all upstairs and then I went out onto the deck, turned on the waterfall and then sat there sipping coffee. I didn't expect that I would be joining the crew upstairs because, quite frankly, in the last twenty-four hours, Bev had drained me dry. I knew I would get the cream pie when everyone was gone, but I seriously doubted that my dick was going to get hard again for a while.

I was feeding the fish when a voice behind me said, "And just how is my favorite cum-sucker today?"

I turned and saw Helen standing there with an extremely tall and well-built blonde. "I brought you what you asked for, sweetie. Cindy is a young housewife with no kids and I left mine with Sandy. So, you have two of us to play with and no interruptions. Best of all, as you should be able to tell from the way I'm talking, Cindy won't need any coffee."

There was a moment of silence and then Helen said, "What's the matter, sweetie? You don't look happy to see us."

"Well I guess that I'm embarrassed because you caught me at a bad time. I don't think that I can perform."

"Bullshit! Take it out, sweetie and let Super Slut Helen at it. I'll have you up in no time and if I can't do it I'll bet that one look at Cindy's naked bod will do it. Go ahead honey, show him the goods."

Cindy looked hesitantly at me and then at Helen. Helen said, "Go ahead, honey. We talked about this and this is what you need. No emotional entanglements, nothing to get in the way of your love for your hubby, just a no frills fuck for the sake of sex."

Cindy glanced nervously at me and then I saw determination in her eyes and she began to unbutton her blouse. Helen said, "This is prime stuff and you owe me big time for getting you first crack at her." Cindy was indeed prime stuff. Six feet tall, 140 pounds and a rack to die for. As Cindy stripped I got the full story from Helen. Cindy had gone to the altar a virgin, got hooked on having sex every day for a year and then the cowboy in the White House had called up Cindy's husband's National Guard unit and had sent him over the big pond to get sand in his shorts. Cindy went from daily to nothing overnight and she hadn't seen or touched a cock in almost six months. Cindy lived next door to Helen and one morning over coffee, Cindy had cried the blues to Helen and Helen had spent the next two weeks convincing Cindy that being a faithful little housewife was a waste of time. "Save your love for your hubby, sweetie, but give your body what it is crying out for." Finally Cindy's sexual frustration had become so overpowering that she had agreed to come with Helen to my place.

Cindy was finally naked and standing in front of me. She was magnificent and I'm ashamed to say that even though my cock twitched a time or two, it just would rise to the occasion. "I'm sorry, ladies, but I'm embarrassed to have to tell you that I can't help you."

Helen gave me a funny look and said, "You're telling me that you can't get it up?"

I opened the bathrobe and displayed my limp manhood and Helen said, "I can take care of that, sweetie." She knelt between my legs and went to work on me. She tried for several minutes and she did manage to get it half hard, but she never got it hard enough that it would penetrate anything. She looked up at me, "What's wrong?"

"Bev has drained me dry."

"When was she here?"

"She got here at eight yesterday morning and she hasn't left yet."

"Bev is here?"

"Yeah. Her husband went out of town for two days. We spent all day yesterday and all last night doing the horizontal bop and she didn't leave me with anything for you girls."

"Where is she?"

"Upstairs with Tyrone and her platoon of Mexican lovers."

Helen looked over at Cindy, "Well, honey, I only intended for you to have sex with stud here, but since he can't, let's go upstairs and see what we can find" and she took Cindy by the hand and led her into the house.

I could have cried. Two great-looking women, no babies to get in the way, and I couldn't get it up. I spent the next half hour sipping coffee and feeding fish and then I went upstairs to see what was going on. Tyrone and Carlos were trying to keep up with Bev and Francisco and Juan were keeping Helen occupied

And Manulito was buried to the hilt in Cindy. I didn't see any more signs of hesitation or reluctance on Cindy's part - all I saw was enthusiasm. It was kind of funny, in an erotic sort of way, watching short, stocky Manulito on top of six foot tall Cindy. With her arms and legs wrapped around Manulito you could hardly even see him. I stood and watched as all five guys sampled Cindy at least once and around two the guys started getting ready to leave. When the guys were gone, Helen said, "Even though you can't get it up, you can still play vacuum cleaner, right?"

***

That was sixteen months ago and a lot has happened since then. Between Sandy and Helen, they brought five more young married mothers into my backyard to see the pond and waterfall and I managed to get three more on my own. Four of them come back from time to time, one of them comes back at least once a week and two of them have never been seen on my end of the street since. One of them still pushes her baby buggy past the front of my house, but on the other side of the street and she never fails to give the house or me the finger as she goes by. None of them ever told their husbands, at least not that I know of, although I suppose there could be one or two husbands out there lying in wait.

It did get a little tight once when one of the women got pregnant and they baby was born black. She ran for her parents and stayed with them until her divorce was final and her husband had split and then one day I came home to find the baby lying on my doorstep. Who was I going to complain to? I named him Andy and I tell people that I adopted him. Derek and Devon are constantly arguing over which of them the kid favors, but I'd put my money on Tyrone.

Bev ran away with Carlos or Juan or maybe both of them.

Cindy stopped by three or four times a week until her husband came home and then she stopped. She did come see me once when he went on a three-day hunting trip, but I haven't seen her now in over six months.

Helen got home one day to find her husband waiting for her demanding to know where she had been. Even though I had cleaned her pussy out before she left my house, she'd taken so much that the crotch of her shorts was soaked and he noticed it. She is living with me now and she has been hinting at marriage. I already know that any wife of mine is going to have to be a slut so she has a foot in the door there, but I can't commit. Why, since she seems so perfect for me? Well, it seems that one day Sandy decided to have a moment of truth. She told her husband that even though she loved him, she needed more sex than he could provide. Then she told him about her gangbangs (but not where she had them-thank God) and he tossed her out on the street. She is also living with me and every time Helen brings up the marriage business, Sandy pipes up with, "Not so fast you round-heeled slut, I saw him first." The two of them are still fucking Tyrone and the boys into the ground and show no signs of ever letting up.

Tyrone's brother wants to join our little group so he can see first-hand how the compound he discovered works, but Ty isn't too keen on the idea. He says his brother is a bit of a tight-ass and he doesn't think he will fit in.

I don't know what I'm going to do with regard to Sandy and Helen, but until I make up my mind there is this sweet looking redhead who has just moved into the neighborhood. She pushes her baby carriage past my house about nine-fifteen every morning. I need to find out how she feels about ponds and waterfalls.

The End

Here is a sample from another story you may enjoy:

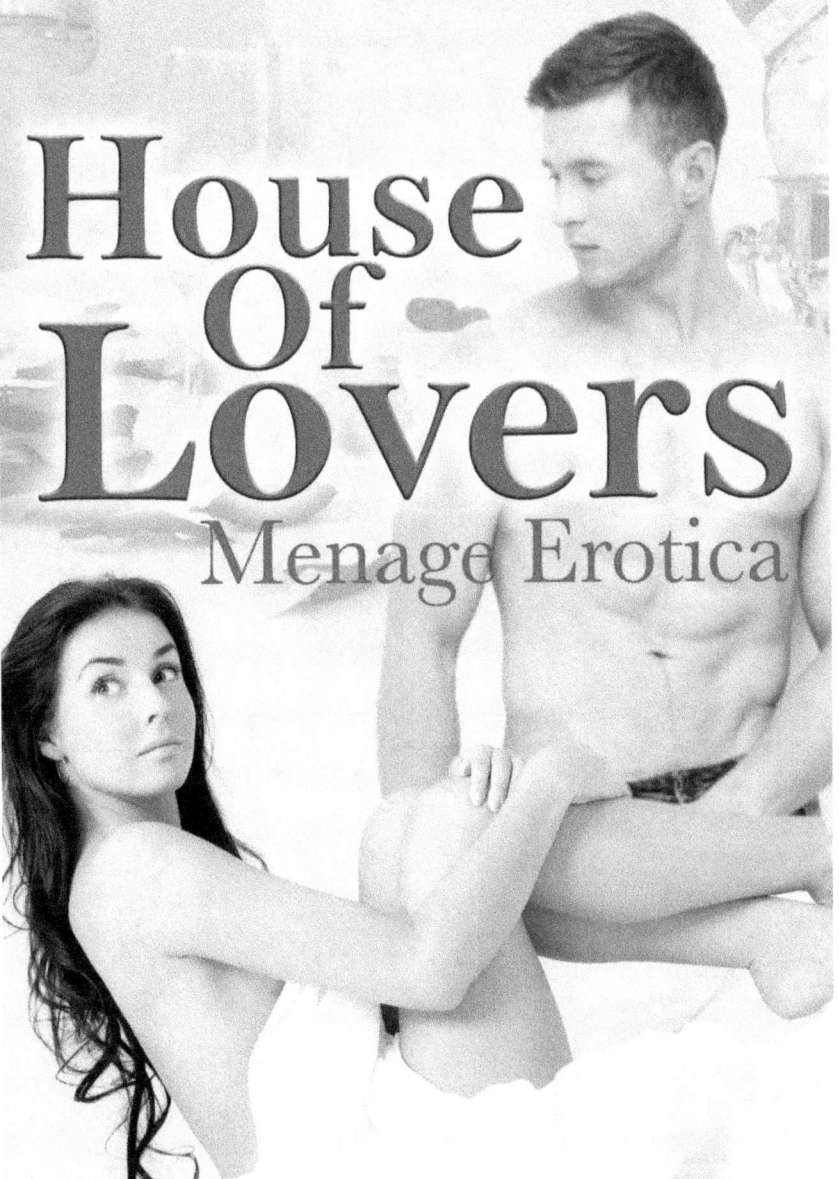

House
Of
Lovers

Menage Erotica

Just Plain Bob

The following year brought me in contact with Mellisa a lot more than I would have liked. Shortly after the start of the New Year, Mr. Banks passed away and Ron succeeded him as president and CEO of the company. By the time that happened I had come to understand that it had been Mr. Banks who had for some strange reason taken an interest in me and who had arranged my "employment contract". Now he was gone and Ron didn't have to suck up to him and I had to wonder if my circumstances might suddenly change. As the months went by and nothing happened, I began to relax a little.

Then Mellisa had another run in with the law that made the papers and Ron decided that it was time that she learned to be a little more responsible. When school let out for the summer he made her go to work at the plant and that put her in almost daily contact with me. She dogged me and hovered around me to the point where everyone in the department was getting a good laugh out of it; everyone except me of course. I was even more acutely aware of the potential for disaster and I worked hard at avoiding her, but she worked just as hard at seeing that I couldn't. Just how hard she was working at it became apparent at the company picnic.

I was eating a hot dog and watching some guys pitch horse shoes when Mellisa came up to me. She didn't say hi, just tugged at my arm and said, "You need to hurry, they are almost ready to start."

"Start what?"

"The Three Legged Race."

"I didn't sign up for the race."

"I know, your partner did it for you."

"Don't tell me, let me guess. You?"

She smiled at me. "Yep."

"Looks like you won't be in the race then."

"No? I already told my dad that you and I were going to win. He will be so disappointed. He does so like to see me succeed. I have no idea how he will react when I tell him that you blew me off."

Daddy had to be happy with a third place finish, but that wasn't bad when you consider that there were thirty-one couples in the race. Ron came up and gave her a hug and congratulated her and she said, "We'll do better in the Wheel Barrow Race, won't we, Ryan?"

As Ron walked away I asked, "Do you have any other surprises for me?"

"Well, after the barrow race there is the balloon race and after that there is the Wrestle."

"The Wrestle? What is that?"

"You'll see, Ryan. Come on, they are lining up for the next race," and she grabbed my hand and pulled me along behind her.

We won the barrow race, but we didn't even come close in the Balloon Race, but then I guess Mellisa never intended to try and win. In the Balloon Race a water-filled balloon is placed between two partners, chest to chest, and without using your arms or hands you have to race from the start to the finish without breaking the balloon or letting it hit the ground. The race started and it became immediately apparent to me what Mellisa was up to. What she intended to do was give me a hard time. The race started and we had gone maybe five feet when suddenly Mellisa stepped back and allowed the balloon to begin to fall. Quickly she moved back in and caught the balloon between our stomachs and this put her tits above the balloon and as she pressed forward to trap the balloon, her tits pressed into my chest. She had a wicked grin on her face and she said, "I'm not wearing a bra, Ryan. Can you feel my nipples touching you?"

I probably didn't, but I imagined that I did and I got an instant woodie. We were fifty feet from the finish line and there was no way I was going to be able to go that distance with her tits rubbing my chest so I did the only thing possible – I stepped forward and pushed. The balloon broke and I found out that I'd only made things worse. The water from the balloon soaked Mellisa's shirt and it had the same as if she had been in a "wet T-shirt" contest.

If you enjoyed this sample then look for **House Of Lovers**.

Also by this Author:

The Prodigal Family: The Abbotts

Watching My Shared Wife

The Waitress and the Runaway Husband

Baiting Mr. Little

Too Hot for Henry

Chuck's Fantasy

The Redhead's Desires

Rescued at Riley's

His Every Fantasy

Open Mike Night

Pursuit for Revenge

Why Does He Do That?

Halloween & Drugs

Tracey

When Rob Met Kari

Becoming a Shared Wife, Vol. 1 –

(Wife Sharing and Other Adventures)

Becoming a Shared Wife, Vol. 2 –

(Hazardous Wives)

Becoming a Shared Wife, Vol. 3 –

(Wives Who Stray)

Becoming a Shared Husband, Vol. 1 –

(Suck Me)

Becoming a Shared Husband, Vol. 2 –

(Husbands Who Stray)

Becoming a Shared Husband, Vol. 3 –

(Get even!)

Becoming a Shared Couple, Vol. 1 –

(Steamy Swingers)

Becoming a Shared Couple, Vol. 2 –

(The Share Thing)

Becoming a Shared Couple, Vol. 3 –

(Kathy is Wild)

Erotica Short Stories, Vol. 1 –

(Taboo Desires)

Erotica Short Stories, Vol. 2 –

(Nasty Steps)

Erotica Short Stories, Vol. 3 –

(Married But...)

Erotica Short Stories, Vol. 4 –

(Sizzling 10)

Erotica Short Stories, Vol. 5 –

(In My Wife's Panties)

Erotica Short Stories, Vol. 6 –

(Taboo Unlimited Desires)

Erotica Short Stories, Vol. 7 –

(XXX Stories)

From the Author

WANT FREE COPIES OF MY BOOKS?

Just visit my blog and download free copies of my books:

awesomeauthors.org/justplainbob

Yes, I write about sluts and whores because as everyone knows, you tend to write about the things you know. And I do like sluts and whores, just not the ones that lie to me and cheat on me.

So be forewarned - if you click on a Just Plain Bob story you will be getting sluts, whores and husbands who do not kill, maim and destroy. There are other things you will rarely find in a Just Plain Bob story.

If you enjoyed any of my books then please share the love and promote my books in Amazon. I would really appreciate your honest reviews, too!

Good news is always welcome.

One Last Thing, For Kindle Readers...

When you turn the page, Kindle will give you the opportunity to rate this book and share your thoughts on Facebook and Twitter. If you enjoyed my writings, would you please take a few seconds to let your friends know about it? Because... when they enjoy they will be grateful to you and so will I.

Thank you!

Just Plain Bob
justplainbob@awesomeauthors.org

You may also like the books by these authors:

Wives
Lend A

HOT EROTICA

Hand

by **LEON RANDALL**

This was a unique occasion in my 56 year life. I was completely naked with a rampant hard-on in the company of my darling wife (who, of course, had seen my extended appendage a million times before) but also in the company of another couple, for whom seeing my erection was a first-time experience. As a group we were transitioning from being just friends to friends plus 'more'. Russell and I were sitting on the sofa in Jan's and my house, a couple of feet apart, each with our hands tucked at our sides so we couldn't touch our dicks. That was the deal we'd agreed to. We were being watched by our wives who were sitting on the ends of the sofa, enjoying our 'situation'. An hour before, this would have been embarrassingly unthinkable. But now, each of us had our Willies about as engorged and scarlet-purple as it's possible to be, both of us were hard and oozing precum and, at least in my case, throbbing and close to a hair trigger which any moment was threatening to see me tip over that edge and come messily all over myself, hands-free and without even being touched. Sound impossible? I would have thought so, too, until that Saturday afternoon.

* * *

We met Eva and Russell via a nudist website. If you've read some of our other stories you'll know how Jan and I fumbled our way into nudism. I won't go into all that again here, but the highly summarised version is that when our son moved out of the house to live-in at university we suddenly found ourselves able to be all frisky again in ways that you really can't be when your kids live at home. I'm pleased to say that Jan and I genuinely still love each other - are still 'in love' might be a nice way to put it - and are enjoying a revitalised sex life with this newly-found empty-nest freedom. To our mutual surprise and enjoyment we have learned a new thing or two about each other's sexual desires as a result (amazing that after years of marriage that can happen, but it can) and discovered we shared some interests in exhibitionism and voyeurism. We'd led an enjoyable but pretty tame sex life until recently so this opened up exciting possibilities - at least in theory. We were both timid about turning those thoughts into reality. We're both possessive of each other and didn't want new and naughty sexual 'fun' to turn out to be not fun at all and leave us jealous or unhappy that we'd gone too far, too fast. In that context, swinging has a tantalising appeal in theory but we agreed neither of us really wanted that so we looked for softer options. We put our toe in the nudism water as a fairly obvious early step. It promised to be a bit naughty but not likely to get us arrested or divorced. And by its nature (no pun intended) it promised to provide chances to see and be seen. We had aspirations for 'more' than just that, but wanted to take it slowly. So, that's how we met with Eva and Russell.

If you enjoyed this sample then look for **<u>Wives Lend A Hand</u>**.

A Compilation of Love Stories

Love and Lust

Erotic Romance

Amy Redek

With our meal over, she said, "This is my bed," pointing to the large palm leaves that I'd already noted, "and you'll have to sleep on the sand tonight. We'll get some more palm leaves tomorrow for you." So with that, she pulled the unburnt wood from the fire and went and settled herself down on the palm leaves, pointing to the sand next to her. So that's where I went and lay down, seeing her settle herself in the dim moonlight before we said our goodnights to each other.

She at least was wearing some sort of clothing whereas I was only wearing my shorts and I woke up sometime during the night feeling quite cold, and I must have rolled over to her to share some of her body heat, for I was cuddled up to her when I awoke in the morning. She must have known this but never said a word as I rolled away from her and got up and walked out onto the beach to see that my boat was still there. I even went and had a swim and on coming back to the shelter, saw that she had set out two small palm leaves that took the place of plates and on each, was a variety of fruit which appeared to be our breakfast.

With that finished, she wanted to show me over the island but I insisted that we salvaged as much as we could from the boat before it disappeared. And so that's how we spent my first full day on the island, by getting everything that I could off the boat. Lunch had just been nuts and fruit but for dinner, we toasted some spam to eat and she didn't really like the fact that I would only open up one can of tinned peaches. Taking it in turns to spoon out a segment to eat and then shared the juice to drink. She thought it was delicious and wished that I would open another but I stood by what I had said from the start that we would be parsimonious with the tinned food to make it last as long as possible.

What with spending the whole day ferrying this from the boat via the sail, we forgot about getting some large palm leaves for my bed and so, like the night before, I was to sleep on the sand again next to her. But like the night before, I was cuddled up to her like two spoons in a drawer, my body up tight to hers with an arm over her and I know damn well that she felt me when I woke up, for I had a massive morning erection and it was pressed up to her backside. I rolled away from her and went straight down to the sea and dived in to let the coolness of the sea to shrink my erection back down to its normal size.

Yet again, she never said a word but it showed when she said that before we tried to salvage more from the boat that we got some big palm leaves for my bed. I'm sure my face went red at her saying this but this is what we did after our breakfast. I am not going to keep repeating myself but breakfast consisted of the same fare every morning, so take it as read as to what we ate having already said what it consisted of.

So with my bed in place next to hers, we went swimming again to get the last of what could be transferred ashore. This was done by the end of the morning, and the afternoon was spent in building up a fire beacon that could be lit on seeing any vessel in sight. The extra advantage was the fact that I still had the Very Light and flares to send up if needed.

Now for dinner, we had plates to eat from and not palm leaves and the tinned chicken stew went down a treat as did the tinned fruit for dessert. The cheese, what I had left over, had now gone so mouldy as to be inedible and she was going to throw it into the sea but I stopped her as it would make good bait, for I had salvage my fishing gear which later came in full use for catching fish to cook and eat. I think I'm dragging this out a bit being somewhat reluctant to say what happened that night, but I suppose I'll have to.

We still had moonlight when we laid down on our palm leaves, me now having a T shirt to wear and not feeling the cold air so much. But it was her that rolled over to me this night and cuddled up to me and had her hand come over my waist. Now just with having her bring her body up to mine set my own body into a state of flux. With me feeling her breasts being up close to my back and her hand over my hip, aroused me, and my body gave out a shiver when her hand felt the front of my shorts. She felt what was there inside, a man's penis at a full erection and knew exactly what to do with it.

Her hand then moved and slowly undid each button on the front and with the front now being open, her hand went inside and...

If you enjoyed this sample then look for **Love And Lust**.

HIS WIFE
and
HER HUSBAND
SPOUSES WHO STRAY

HOT ROMANCE EROTICA
JACK RYDER

Shelly and I were always sort of mismatched now that I look back at the eight years we were husband and wife. I was always a night owl. Preferring the late night hours to write my stories when there were no distractions and the rest of the neighborhood was asleep.

Shelly was one of those early to rise and early to bed sorts. She spent her morning working out to keep her highly tuned body at its peak performance. She spent the rest of her day with her clients. Shelly was a very popular personal trainer in our little part of the world.

Things went fairly well the first three or four years of our relationship. We could laugh off our differences as amusing quirks that added to the uniqueness of our love. But after a while, those differences began to grate on us. It began to erode the foundation of that uniqueness.

Shelly was always so busy that she often left things a mess. It wasn't just a little mess either. She would leave any room she'd been in looking like a tornado had roared through. After years of cleaning up after her, I began to resent it. I felt like I was her personal maid or something.

It seemed that Shelly's biggest resentment was that I would try to get sexual with her when she was ready for bed. But she grew more and more resistant as the years went by. Often telling me she was too tired or that it pissed her off that I would get back up afterward to go do some more writing.

After a while, we fell into a routine of sorts. I stopped complaining about her messiness but became very quiet and uncommunicative when she was home. She responded by coming home later and later and curtailing our sex life to a holiday treat or as a favor when she wanted something special. Those episodes usually occurred each time I received a large bonus when one of my books did very well.

I'm sort of telling you all this boring stuff so you can get an idea of how we sort of drifted our own directions. I became accustomed to doing pretty much whatever I wanted to go do. And Shelly pretty much came and went as she pleased as well.

But you need to understand that I never once considered having an affair or seeking out companionship in any manner. I truly believed that we were just suffering through growing pains and that eventually things would straighten out for us.

I also have to tell you that I have a very active sexual drive. As time passed, I found ways to…take care of my own needs so to speak. I found ways to satisfy myself. I found there were many ways that one could have anonymous sex and there were many others that were seeking the same release.

It started out with a few harmless trips to the Adult Arcade out on the edge of town. The sign had just caught my eye one afternoon after having an argument with Shelly. She had taunted me afterward saying that the next time she would fuck me is when pigs fly.

I felt a little apprehensive when I first stepped into the arcade. Afraid I might see someone that I know and they would think I was some sort of pervert. I was surprised to see that there were nearly a dozen people milling around in the large center area that was filled with rows of videos, sex toys and sexy lingerie.

I noticed a couple of men over in the back corner by the gay magazine row. They seemed to be sizing me up as they gawked at the magazines they were holding. It even appeared that two of them were sort of petting each other below the level of the shelves.

There were a couple of middle age women that seemed like they were a little embarrassed to be here. But they were whispering requests at the counter clerk.

I figured they were here to purchase some stuff to spice up their sex life at home. I felt a little jealous as I thought of that. At least these women were trying to find ways to keep their sex life alive.

I also noticed one woman in the other back corner alone. She was holding up sexy panties as if inspecting them. But she kept looking over as if to see if I was paying attention to her. She was wearing a very short mini skirt and extremely tight pull over top. The way her nipples were poking against the tight cotton fabric, it was easy to tell she was not wearing a bra. She sort of looked like a hooker.

I noticed the hall way to the arcade with the private booths. I smiled at the woman one last time then made my way down the hall. I went to the very last booth at the far end of the hall and closed the door behind me. I quickly shoved $5 in the pay slot and selected a porn video to watch.

I just got my pants down and was gently tugging on my prick when I heard the door to the booth next to mine open and close. Moments later, I heard the sound of the machine taking money in the next booth. Then I heard a loud moaning as the porn came on in the next booth. In a few seconds, the sound became the same as the video that I was watching.

I was just getting a good rhythm to my jerking when I suddenly heard "Pssssst," coming from the wall next to me. When I glanced down, I saw a four inch hole in the wall at just the same level as my cock...

If you enjoyed this sample then look for <u>His Wife And Her Husband</u>.

SAVING
Heather

HOT ROMANCE EROTICA
LILITH JONES

She went into his arms. Her kiss had been intended to be a light acceptance of his niceness. He kept it up, though, and she certainly had no reason to end it. He sucked her lower lip, and then he licked her lips. She opened them to him, but he kept licking them. She finally sought his tongue with hers. When they met, sparks flew. He pulled her to him, and she felt his firmness against her stomach.

"Oh, my love," he said when they broke. His hands went to the buttons on her blouse. She was his, and she let him strip her. He did it slowly, kissing every newly revealed inch of skin. She felt aroused, more aroused than she had been in years. She also felt cherished, cherished as not even the Rick of years ago had cherished her.

When he was kneeling and he had her jeans down around her ankles, he eased back to let her step out of them. Then he kissed her legs upward to her panties. He kissed her mound through those panties, and she felt ready for him. He eased her down on the bed.

If he'd been patience personified in removing her clothes, he was nearly a blur in removing his. Then he faced her, fully nude and magnificently male. He looked as ready for her as she felt ready for him. She pushed the panties down, and Rick took them off her feet. She spread her legs slightly as he got into bed.

He started with a kiss, though. It was a gentle, but extremely sensual, kiss. She arched her hips off the bed as their tongues met. He cupped her, holding all her femininity. As he moved his mouth from hers to her breasts, her nipple strained upward towards his mouth. He licked it, touching only the tip with the tip of his tongue. She quivered all over, and he moved to the other breast. When he sucked that nipple, sparks shot from the tips of her toes.

He thrust one finger deep inside her. Then he drew it out, very slowly, and over her clit. It was only one finger, but it went so slowly that it felt much more -- maybe a yard long. He changed breasts again and sucked deeply. The sucking and the stroking were sending heat through her. She felt as though she was being baked, and there was a fire in her womb.

He raised his head from her breast and stared into her eyes. "Heather," he said. "Heather, my love."

Then lightning crackled within her. She moaned and writhed. It went on as he kept stroking. She collapsed, and he removed his finger. He kissed her forehead and her shoulder. As her breath eased, he kissed her nose tip, and then her breasts, and then her stomach.

He again stroked her mound. He rubbed the lips there against one another, very softly. The response, however, was fire. His hand was wonderful, and his look was loving if it was searching. He had brought her delight, and she could believe he would bring her more delight. She wanted more than that, though.

"You," she said. "Please!" He rolled away suddenly. She stifled a protest when she saw that he was reaching in his drawer. She almost told him that he didn't need the rubber. She could tell, though, that this was one more act of caring. He was taking responsibility, taking care of her. Whatever the physical shortcomings, she would celebrate it as an action of the man who would never put her at risk.

Now, he was kneeling between her legs. She spread her lips with her hand and rolled her hips to receive him fully. She felt open to him.

"Heather," he said.

"Yes, oh yes."

However open she had been, she felt him stretch her more as he went in slowly. And it was slow, agonizingly slow. When he had filled her, he kissed her briefly. She hugged him with her arms and with her legs. He was in her, but she wanted to hold all of him.

He withdrew as slowly, and he felt a need for him to return. He thrust in a little faster, and she felt herself burn. As he sped up, it was never fast enough. She thrust up to engulf him as he came down. Then the lightning crashed through her again.

He withdrew half way, rammed into her, and pulsed deep within her. For a second, he was one rigid arch within her hug. Then he collapsed onto his elbows. She, too, relaxed. Her feet rested on his calves, and her hands rested on his back, but she was no longer really hugging him.

That was closeness. They were one. She was disappointed when he moved away, although the freedom to breathe was a relief. He moved off the bed and turned off the overhead light. As he came back, she heard the rubber drop into the wastebasket.

"We really need another pillow," he said as he got into bed. He lay down beside her and pulled her into a hug. He carefully spread the sheet over both of them.

"We don't really need a wider bed, though," she said. He chuckled. "Y'know . . . Maybe you don't know. I'm on the pill."

"Well, it didn't seem a good time to ask."

"It wasn't. You took care of me."

"I always will," he said. "Somebody should. You work too hard taking care of Anne. Somebody has to take care of you."

"Well, maybe, we'll take care of each other."

"That's a good idea. I love you. Seriously, if we're going to be a family, we'll have to divide up the family tasks. Probably, you should do the dividing. But give me some of the tasks of caring for Anne. Just because I don't know how, doesn't mean I can't learn."

"You do great. I might have to give her the baths and wash her clothes, but you give her kisses and protect her."

"Washing her clothes and yours can't be all that different from washing mine, and I wash mine already. Anyway, first you get the divorce, preferably with full custody. Next we get married. Then, if I can, I adopt her. After that, we'll try to get her to call me Daddy."

"I love you." Heather thought Rick's project to get Anne to call him Daddy reflected more of the story that she'd heard at the funeral than Anne's situation. Right now, Anne had two men in her life. One beat her, and she called him Daddy. The other hugged her, and she called him Rick. Anne would know which name meant love. Well, courts took forever, and four-year-olds were resilient. By the time Rick had gone through his agenda, Anne would call him anything he wanted.

"And I love you, too," Rick said. She believed him. His hand stroked up to her breast, and she patted it and held it there. "Is this what married people do?" he asked. "I mean lie in bed and talk later?"

"Well, I'm not sure that I want my last marriage to be a model." And that was an understatement. Too many of her conversations with Bill had been at the top of their lungs. "Is this what you want our marriage to be?"

"Yeah. Especially this part." He squeezed her breast very lightly. "I like holding you."

"And," she said in satisfaction, "I like being held by you."

If you enjoyed this sample then look for Saving Heather.

DEXTER'S
Renaissance

LEE NORTH

Hot Romance Erotica

That May picnic was the beginning of a series of dates that Michelle and I enjoyed. Sometimes to a movie or play, often for dinner, occasionally for a ballgame. It was on one of those dates that there was a distinct shift in our relationship. Until then, we had held hands, kissed lightly, and generally behaved ourselves. I think we both could feel the pressure building. It changed after we had spent a pleasant evening at a local play.

We were in her late model Lincoln and I was driving. In the past, I would stop at the Rossmoor and she would drive on to her apartment. That night she had other ideas.

"Drive to my place, Dex. It's Friday, and we've got all weekend. You haven't been to my place yet and I'd like to spend some time with you," she said, placing her hand over mine.

It didn't take me any time at all to agree and head toward Lakeshore Drive. As we neared the building, Michelle took a small transmitter from her purse and pushed a button. The open grilled gate began to rise and I drove into the underground parking area as she directed me to her numbered space. The transmitter also unlocked the door to the elevator and stairs. After waiting a moment for an available car, a door slid open and we entered with Michelle inserting a card and pushing a button marked "R."

When we stepped out of the car, a large glass window was directly in front of us and I could see we were at the top of the building. To the left was 2102 and to the right, 2101. Michelle guided me right and opened the door, stepping in and turning on some lights.

It was a very nice and apparently large penthouse suite, one of two on the top floor of the building. As I looked around I saw the trappings of affluence; fine furniture, interesting artwork, and lush carpeting.

Michelle kicked off her shoes and I followed suit.

"Dex, I'm all sticky from the humidity today. I'm going to have a shower and change. Why don't you do the same, then we can relax and get to know each other better," she smiled.

I wasn't about to decline the offer and happily agreed. She led me to the main bathroom, handed me some towels and a washcloth and told me how to work the controls on the shower system. I needed the lesson. It was a multi-head system with pre-selected temperatures. The cabinet itself was almost as big as the bathroom in my apartment.

As I soaped and rinsed, I almost expected that Michelle would suddenly appear and join me, but that didn't happen. I stepped out of the shower, towelled myself off, and dressed in my slacks and shirt. I didn't bother with socks. They wouldn't be as fresh as I was so I stuffed them in my back pocket as I headed barefoot for the living area.

Waiting for Michelle, I wandered about the spacious penthouse. There was a dining area with a very nice buffet and china cabinet, along with a large period-style table and chairs. The kitchen was through a wide passage and it too was large, with a big island and plenty of cabinet and counter space. Most houses didn't have this much room.

I was just coming out of my inspection of the kitchen when Michelle reappeared and got my undivided attention. She was wearing a black silk pyjama suit, if that's what it's called. It was floor length, very sleek with material flowing from its wide legs and arms. She had a smile for me as she approached, then stopped and swirled in a circle to emphasize the graceful lines of her attire.

"You like?" she asked, already knowing my answer.

"Very nice ... very elegant." I almost added very sexy. As she had moved to show off the garment it was immediately apparent that she was wearing nothing beneath it. Her nipples protruded clearly in front and her buttocks were perfectly outlined in back. I could feel my erection beginning to develop.

"Would you care for coffee ... or perhaps a glass of wine or brandy?" she asked in a tempting tone.

"I'd like a glass of brandy, please."

"Oh, good. I'll have one too," she said, turning to move into the kitchen.

I followed her as if she was drawing me along. Perhaps it was the magnetic appeal of her, dressed as she was in such alluring garb. She reached up in a cupboard for the brandy bottle and I stepped behind her to help her. I was directly behind her now, touching her slightly with my hips and chest. On the spur of the moment, I did something I would never have thought I would do.

With the fingertips of my right hand, I lightly, slowly, ran them up her side, feeling her ribs as I went. Then, in a moment of complete recklessness, I moved my hand and gently cupped and stroked a fulsome breast. I felt her shiver from the contact but she didn't push me away or resist my touch. In fact, I was sure I heard a soft moan.

I couldn't see her face, but she had begun to lean back into me, the brandy bottle now forgotten. Her hands were on the countertop as if bracing her against an assault. My left hand joined the right in teasing her nipples and now her groan was more audible. Emboldened, I allowed my left hand to slip down over her abdomen and softly rub the silky smooth material of her gown.

I felt her backside push slowly back into me and she could certainly now feel my erection. I moved my hips to place my hardened member between her cheeks. She welcomed that with a swaying motion that only reinforced my hardness. One of us was going to have to do something soon.

It was Michelle who took my right hand and guided it inside her top, giving me access to her breasts. She pulled at the fold of the material and I felt a little pop as a small snap released the upper half of the garment. Still holding my hand, she slid it down to her waist where another small snap gave way and the gown parted completely.

I felt her shrug her shoulders and the lovely black item fell at her feet. She was naked before me, still facing away but leaning back more urgently against me, pressing herself into my prominent manhood. Once more, I did something I would not have thought I could attempt. I intimated with my knee that I wanted her to spread her legs and she immediately complied. She understood exactly what I was intending.

I unbuttoned my pants and they too fell at my feet, my briefs following them almost immediately. I took my cock in my hand and began to stroke her already wet centre in preparation for my entry. Again, she did everything she could to help me and within a few moments I was pushing into her. Slowly and carefully at first, but her insistence gave me courage to thrust a little more and soon I was buried well inside her.

I moved a little more forcefully and quickly as she continued to encourage me. There was absolutely no doubt in my mind that this was what she had planned all along. Her voice soon joined the action, not so much with words but with little cries of encouragement and pleasure. How long it had been since she had been with a man I did not know. I only knew she was with me now, and I was reaping the reward of her pent up need.

I leaned my head forward and captured an earlobe between my lips, then licked the back of her neck as I continued to stroke into her. In response, she threw her head back, growling a pagan, earthy moan of lust, slamming her ass back into me, the smacking sound of our joining now growing louder. This was probably going to end quite soon, but I did whatever I could to hold off as long as possible.

A few moments later her moves became more erratic and we almost fell out of rhythm as she began her orgasmic journey. I stayed with her as long as I could, but I was going to finish as well and there was nothing I could do to prevent it. I felt myself release into her once, twice, then a third time. As I did, she sagged against me and I wrapped my arms around her waist so that she didn't collapse against the granite counter or on the floor.

In all my experience, limited as it might have been, I had never had a more erotic, spontaneous coupling than this. I was in no condition to continue. Michelle was leaning back into me, breathing heavily and holding my arms tightly as they encircled her. Not a word had passed between us from the time she walked to the liquor cupboard.

I'm still not sure what got into me that night. I was either very confident of myself or very reckless. Probably the latter. Nonetheless, I picked the naked beauty up in my arms and carefully steered my way out of the kitchen toward the master bedroom. When I arrived, I saw that the bed had been turned down and I carefully laid Michelle on it crosswise with her legs dangling over the side. Her eyes were open and she was staring at me, no doubt wondering what I was doing. Still, neither of us had yet spoken.

I pulled off my shirt and now as naked as she, I got on my knees on the lushly carpeted floor, my hands gently but insistently pushing her legs apart. Again, she offered no resistance. I moved between her thighs and began to kiss the flawless, smooth skin. I was about to work my way up to the place where I had just planted my seed when I felt her hands in my hair. Was this a 'stop' or a 'go?'

I could see a bit of my semen on the lips of her vagina and I wondered what possessed me to try this. What was I trying to prove? Yet, even with that question in my head, I continued. As Michelle realized what I was planning, she must have had second thoughts. That had prompted her to place her hands on my head again, trying to decide if she should put a stop to my intentions. As I made up my mind to continue, I felt her resistance lessen.

I moved toward my target and slowly, with the flat of my tongue, I began to make love to her once again. This was going to be a very different kind of penetration. I had plenty of experience with oral sex but none just after I had planted my seed inside a woman. It was too late to stop now, and Michelle was making no sign that she wanted me to.

In fact, I was bringing her back to life with my tongue and fingers. Her hips were rising and falling erratically, responding to whatever stimuli she felt. Her grip on my head tightened and I could feel her fingers in my hair. She was holding on tight, her body dancing to whatever music my tongue created. I flicked the tip of her clitoris and got the response I expected. Her hips snapped up in reaction.

I was beginning to tire ... or at least my tongue was. Michelle was nearing another orgasm and I willed myself to continue. At last she let go and I could stop and rest. I crawled up beside her, lying on my back. She rolled over me and gave me a deep, soulful kiss. Whatever I had accomplished, she approved of it. I wondered if it was something her late husband had not provided.

We lay there for a while, her head on my shoulder, our legs dangling over the edge of the bed. I kissed her forehead and ran my fingers through her soft, flowing hair. Her hand was holding my now flaccid cock, not manipulating it, just holding it lightly.

"That was wonderful," she said at last. "I didn't realize just how much I wanted you and you were perfect for me."

"We took some chances tonight," I said. "That gown didn't leave much to the imagination."

"It was either that or I would just come out naked. It was a coin toss."

"Were you worried I wouldn't get the message?"

"That thought did cross my mind. I can never be sure just what you are thinking about when it comes to women, Dex. Sometimes shy, but tonight a completely different person. You took command and I was the lucky one when you did."

"You were irresistible. I'm sure that was your plan, wasn't it? Well, it worked. I couldn't resist you, so everything that happened was a result of that."

"You'll stay tonight, won't you?"

"Yes. You might regret it in the morning, but I do want to stay. I want to wake up with you."

"We've started something, haven't we?" It was as much a statement as a question.

"I hope so. Is that what you want?" I wondered.

"Yes. As little as I know about you, as little time as I've known you, everything I've learned tells me that you are right for me."

"Well, we're going to have some time to find out so let's enjoy ourselves and see where it goes. I'm not a one-night-stand kind of guy. I'm looking for something more than that."

"You wouldn't be in this apartment tonight if I thought otherwise. But now that you're here, I'm going to keep you here as long as I can."

After a few minutes, Michelle rose and padded to the ensuite bathroom, closing the door behind her. She returned a minute or so later and crawled on top of me, rubbing my still limp cock with her lightly haired sex. I began to respond to her tantalizing little game and she noticed.

"Oh ... isn't that nice. Can I have some more please, sir?"

"Of course you may. Just tell me your heart's desire, young lady, and I'll try and fulfill your wishes."

"Well, after that glorious fucking you gave me in the kitchen, I think I'd like you to make love to me. Something nice and slow and lasting."

"How would you like me to start? A little foreplay, perhaps?"

"I think I've had all the foreplay I can handle tonight, Dex. I'm still carrying some of you around in me and what I really want is to have you inside me again."

If you enjoyed this sample then look for **Dexter's Renaissance.**

WANT FREE COPIES OF MY BOOKS?
Just visit my blog and download free copies of my books:
awesomeauthors.org/justplainbob

www.ingramcontent.com/pod-product-compliance
Lightning Source LLC
Chambersburg PA
CBHW071417170626
46811CB00003B/1439